This book is dedicated to the greatest quarterback
of them all—Johnny Unitas. —M. L.

The author would also like to give special recognition to William Gildea
and his excellent work, *When the Colts Belonged to Baltimore*, for inspiring this story.

For my father John, "The Brave O'Leary" —C. O.

Text © 2008 by Mike Leonetti.

Illustrations © 2008 by Chris O'Leary.

All rights reserved.

Book design by Jennifer Lacy Bagheri.

Typeset in Lino Letter and Gatlin.

The illustrations in this book were rendered in

acrylic paint on Arches watercolor paper.

Manufactured in China.

Library of Congress Cataloging-in-Publication Data

Leonetti, Mike, 1958–

In the pocket : Johnny Unitas and me / by Mike Leonetti ; illustrated by Chris O'Leary.

p. cm.

Summary: Billy dreams of playing quarterback for the Colts one day, like Johnny Unitas,
and although his coach insists he play receiver until he is bigger, Billy is inspired to try
harder after meeting his hero and seeing the Colts win the 1958 National Football League
championship. Includes biographical information about Unitas.

Includes bibliographical references.

ISBN 978-0-8118-5661-4

[1. Football—Fiction. 2. Unitas, Johnny, 1933–2002—Fiction. 3. Baltimore Colts (Football team)—
History—Fiction. 4. Family life—Maryland—Baltimore—Fiction. 5. Baltimore (Md.)—History—
20th century—Fiction.] I. O'Leary, Chris, ill. II. Title.

PZ7.L5513In 2008

[Fic]—dc22

2007019992

10 9 8 7 6 5 4 3 2 1

Chronicle Books LLC

680 Second Street, San Francisco, California 94107

www.chroniclekids.com

IN THE POCKET

★ ★ ★ ★ ★ ★ ★ ★ ★ ★ ★ ★ ★ ★ ★ ★

Johnny Unitas and Me

By **MIKE LEONETTI**

Illustrated by **CHRIS O'LEARY**

chronicle books · san francisco

The day I had been waiting for was finally here. My father and I were taking the train from Baltimore to New York City to see our team, the Baltimore Colts, play the New York Giants for the National Football League championship. New York was so big compared with Baltimore—tall buildings seemed to touch the sky! The late-December skies were gray, and the weather was mild. I was hoping that would help the Colts throw the ball.

When we got off the train, my dad and I met my uncle Matt and took the subway to Yankee Stadium. Uncle Matt lived in New York and was a Giants fan. He got Dad and me our tickets, but he was going to sit with the Giants fans during the game!

Back home, Dad and I went to practically every Colts home game at Memorial Stadium on 33rd Street. When I couldn't get to the games, I followed the Colts in the newspaper or on the radio or watched them on TV. I knew all the best players, like Raymond Berry, Alan Ameche, Lenny Moore, Jim Parker, Gino Marchetti, and Art Donovan. But the greatest Colt of them all was my hero, quarterback Johnny Unitas.

Johnny Unitas was simply a great passer. Something about the way he threw the ball made almost every pass perfect. He hit the receiver almost every time. And he always kept the other team guessing.

Johnny would stand in the pocket as long as he could before throwing the ball. He was always cool under pressure, and never screamed or hollered at his teammates. Under his leadership, the Colts always had a chance to win the game!

His playing wasn't all that made Johnny stand out. He wore black high-tops and had a brush cut that you couldn't miss when he took his helmet off. But most of all, he inspired me to play football.

Dad was teaching me how to throw a spiral so I could hit receivers just like Johnny. Even though I was a bit on the thin side, I was determined to be a great quarterback. I could run and scramble whenever I was being chased. All I needed was an arm, and I'd have what it takes.

Every chance I got, I played football with my best friend, Tommy, who lived a few doors down from me. He liked to catch and run the ball like Raymond Berry, the best receiver on the Colts. Saturdays we would play all day long! When we played with other boys in the neighborhood, Tommy and I made sure we were always on the same team. We dreamed about playing for the Colts one day.

ommy and I played on a football team for the first time that year, but I didn't get to play quarterback much at all.

One day I pleaded with Coach Barnes to put me in at QB.

"I can throw the ball pretty well, Coach," I said. "And I can avoid getting sacked because I move quickly."

"I know how much you want to be quarterback, son," said Coach Barnes. "But you're not ready yet. Get a little meat on your bones and work on that arm. Maybe next year we'll look at you for quarterback."

We had a decent season: four losses and four wins. But the Colts had a great season, even though Johnny got hurt and had to miss a couple of games. Some of their victories were really lopsided: They beat Detroit 40–14, won 34–7 against Los Angeles, and shut out Green Bay 56–0, for a season total of 9 wins, 3 losses. Dad and I saw the Colts clinch the NFL Western Conference in Baltimore when they beat the San Francisco 49ers in November. The 49ers were up 27–7 at halftime, but the Colts staged a great comeback to win the game 35–27, with Unitas and Lenny Moore leading the way.

Watching Johnny lead the Colts back from behind in that game was so exciting I was even more convinced that I wanted to be my team's quarterback. But how was I going to do it?

The day after the 49ers game, Tommy came running up to my house after school.

"Hey, Billy! I know where one of the Colts lives!" he yelled.

"Which player is it?" I asked excitedly, running out to the porch.

"You'll see when we get there. Bring your football, and grab a pen!" Tommy said breathlessly.

"I don't know if I can go out, Tommy," I said. "I just got my report card, and it wasn't great. Mom and Dad think I'm spending too much time worrying about football and not enough time hitting the books."

"But this is a chance to meet one of the Colts!" Tommy insisted. "Ask your Mom if you can go. We won't be long."

"OK, I'll try," I said. "But don't be surprised if she says no."

I went back into the house, but I didn't need to say anything. Mom had been listening the whole time.

"Billy, with your grades, you know you shouldn't even be thinking about football," she said. My heart sank.

"But it's just a few blocks from here and I'll get back soon to do my homework," I pleaded.

"Well . . ."

She looked serious, but I could tell she was thinking it over.

"You've worked very hard this week, so I'll make this exception. Just be sure to get back in time for dinner. Then it's right back to your homework."

I hugged her. "Thanks, Mom!"

I grabbed my football and ran out the door.

Tommy and I ran for almost four blocks, until we came to Cold Spring Street. It was lined with redbrick houses, and we walked up to one of the homes.

Tommy, always fearless, went right ahead and rang the doorbell.

"Who lives here?" I asked Tommy again. But before he could answer, the door opened. I couldn't believe it! It was Johnny Unitas!

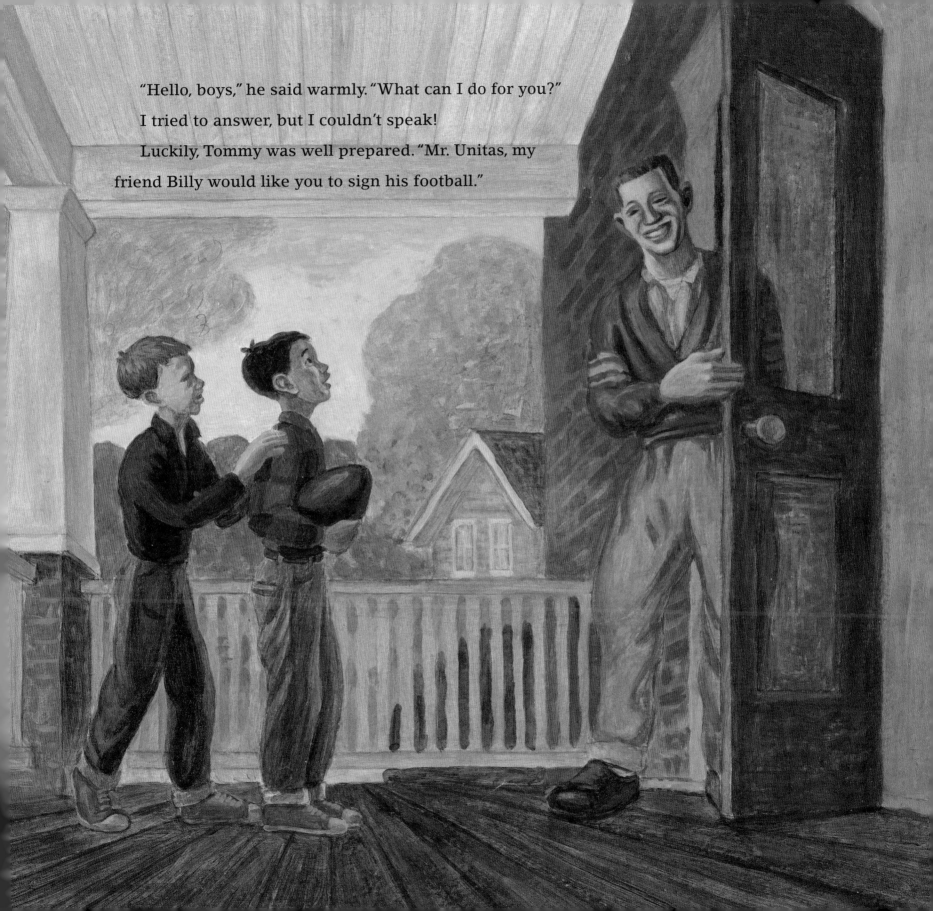

"Hello, boys," he said warmly. "What can I do for you?"
I tried to answer, but I couldn't speak!
Luckily, Tommy was well prepared. "Mr. Unitas, my
friend Billy would like you to sign his football."

Johnny stepped outside and took the football. "Think fast, son," he said as he threw me a pass. I somehow managed to catch it and throw it back to him.

"Hey, good arm, Billy," he said. I couldn't believe it! Johnny Unitas thought I could throw!

"Mr. Unitas, I want to play quarterback just like you," I said, not wanting to miss my chance to talk to my hero. "But my coach won't give me a chance."

"Well, Billy, don't give up. It's not always easy to get something you really want. Look at my career. When I was your age, I was the smallest boy in my class. When I applied to college, none of the big schools wanted me, but I made the most of my time at the University of Louisville. After college, the Pittsburgh Steelers drafted me, but they let me go before I played a single game. I took a job working construction, and played semi-pro ball at night. I never gave up my dream of playing in the NFL. Eventually, the Colts gave me a chance."

"Wow," I said. "I thought you were always a star."

"Not at all. In fact, in the first game I played for Baltimore, the first pass I threw was intercepted and returned for a touchdown! And later in that same game I fumbled the ball! But I stuck with it, and my teammates helped me out," he said. "I wouldn't be where I am without them."

"Do you have any other advice for us, Mr. Unitas?" Tommy said, jumping into the conversation.

"Sure. Get yourself a good education." Johnny said. "There's more to life than just football, and not everyone can make the NFL. A college education is something you can use for a long time."

"My mom will be glad to hear you said that, Mr. Unitas," I chimed in. "Any advice about playing quarterback?"

"Practice throwing every day. When you throw a pass, toss it hard so it gets there fast. That will make it difficult to intercept. Most of all, stick with it. You never know how far you can go," Johnny answered.

"Thanks, Mr. Unitas. I sure hope the Colts win the championship," I said as we were leaving.

"Me too, Billy. See you, boys," Johnny called.

All the way home I clutched the football Johnny
signed. Tommy wanted to toss it around, but there
was no way I was going to smudge Johnny's
autograph! Dad was going to have to buy me a
new football—this one was going to my room
for safekeeping—right next to the issue of *Sport*
magazine with the picture of Johnny Unitas on the
cover and my Unitas trading card.

For the rest of the football season I kept up with my schoolwork, and now Dad and I were about to see the Colts play in the NFL championship game!

"Dad, do you think the Colts can do it?" I asked.

"I think they can, Billy, but it won't be easy. The Giants defense allowed only 183 points all season long; they're the best in the NFL," Dad said, trying to keep me from getting my hopes too high.

"That's right," added Uncle Matt. "The Giants have many good defensive players, like Sam Huff, Rosey Grier, Andy Robustelli, and Emlen Tunnell. They also have experienced players on offense, like Charley Conerly, Kyle Rote, and Frank Gifford."

"Uncle Matt, we have Johnny Unitas on our team, and he won't let us down," I said confidently.

Dad and I said good-bye to Uncle Matt and went to our seats.

The Giants got the first points of the game when Pat Summerall kicked a field goal, giving New York a 3–0 lead. But by halftime, the Colts were up 14–3 on a touchdown run by Ameche and a 15-yard pass to Berry. The New York crowd was hushed.

Just before the start of the third quarter, I turned to Dad. "If the Colts get an early score in the second half, it'll be all over," I said.

"You could be right, Billy."

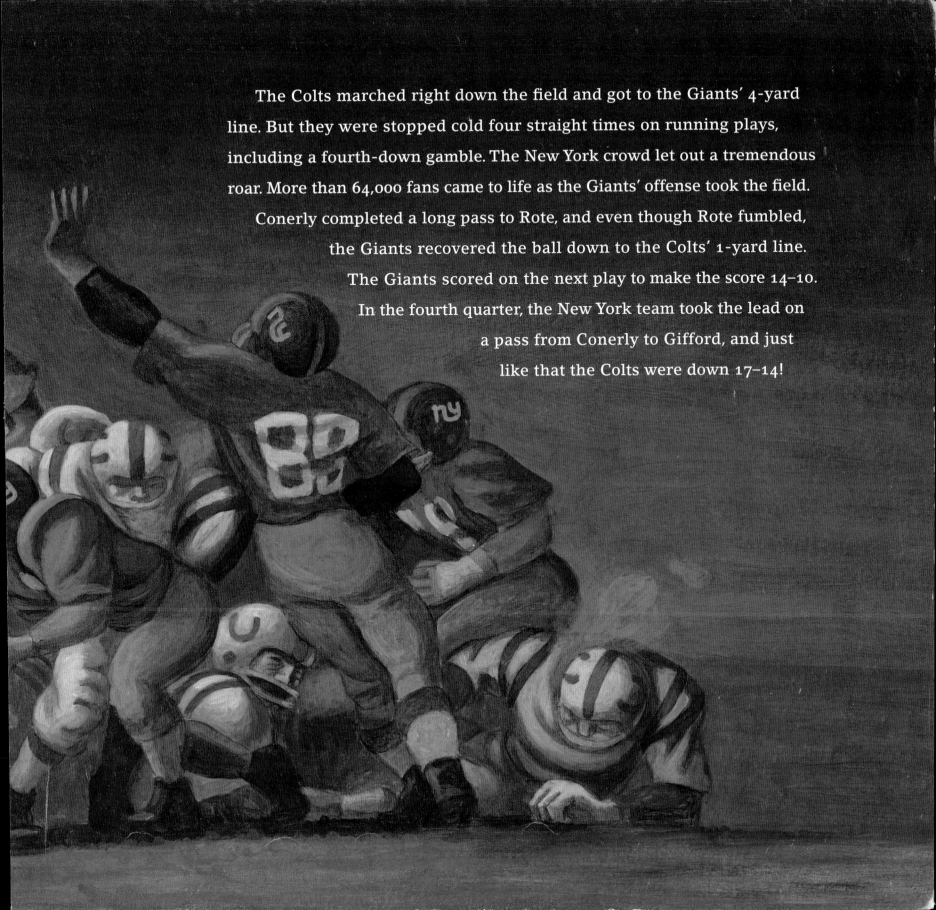

The Colts marched right down the field and got to the Giants' 4-yard line. But they were stopped cold four straight times on running plays, including a fourth-down gamble. The New York crowd let out a tremendous roar. More than 64,000 fans came to life as the Giants' offense took the field. Conerly completed a long pass to Rote, and even though Rote fumbled, the Giants recovered the ball down to the Colts' 1-yard line. The Giants scored on the next play to make the score 14–10. In the fourth quarter, the New York team took the lead on a pass from Conerly to Gifford, and just like that the Colts were down 17–14!

I couldn't believe what was happening! With less than six minutes left to play, the Colts were forced to punt the ball away. The Giants almost made a first down, but Marchetti and Donovan stopped Gifford before he could make it. The Giants decided to punt, and the Colts got the ball back with just about two minutes to play, but they were 86 yards from the New York end zone!

"The only man who can get the Colts out of this situation is Johnny Unitas. He's great in the last two minutes of play," Dad reminded me.

On third down, Unitas hit Moore. Then he found Berry for the next three straight passes. Berry ran precise patterns, and Johnny hit him accurately each time. It looked like they were in complete control. Time was running out. The Colts lined up for a field goal to tie the game. I couldn't look as the Colts' kicker Steve Myhra set up for the kick.

"He made it!" Dad cried. The contest was now even: 17–17.

"What happens now, Dad?" I asked.

"Sudden-death overtime," he said. "The first team that scores wins."

It was colder and darker now, and the stadium lights shone brightly.

The Giants started overtime with the ball, but the Colts stopped them after three plays. They got the ball back on their own 20-yard line and got going with good runs by L. G. Dupre, and a pass to Ameche. Then Johnny was sacked. It looked as if the Colts might have to kick it away until Johnny hit Berry with a pass for a first down. Ameche rumbled up the middle for 23 yards. Johnny completed two more passes, and the Colts were down to the Giants' 1-yard line—right in front of us!

"Why don't they kick a field goal, Dad?" I asked.

"I think the Colts want to win it with a touchdown," Dad guessed.

On the very next play, Unitas handed off to Ameche, who lowered his head and protected the ball. Lenny Moore threw a great block, and there was a huge hole for Ameche to run through.

Touchdown, Colts!

The Colts were NFL champions!

Dad and I took the train
back to Baltimore that night and
ate in the dining car. The whole way
home all we talked about was the Colts' victory.

"You know, Dad, I really learned something today," I said.

"What is that, Billy?"

"Johnny Unitas is right. Look how he played tonight. Even though his team was down and
time was running out, he didn't give up. He got the Colts back into a position to win the game,"
I said with great admiration. "I can't give up either. I am going to make quarterback."

While I waited for the next season to start, I threw the football around every chance I got. When Tommy and Dad weren't around, I'd get Mom to catch a few! I drank lots of milk and tried to eat the right foods to get bigger and stronger. By the time tryouts rolled around I had put on a little weight and I was ready.

At the first practice, Coach Barnes asked those of us who wanted to try out for quarterback to throw the ball as far as we could. Whoever threw the farthest would have the best chance of being the quarterback.

I watched the other boys take their turns, and they made some nice tosses. Then it was my turn. I reared my arm back just like Johnny Unitas did when he was about to make a pass. I heaved the football as hard as I possibly could and it sailed farther than anyone else's!

Suddenly, everything seemed possible!

About

JOHNNY UNITAS

JOHNNY UNITAS

QUARTERBACK   BALTIMORE COLTS

Johnny Unitas was born on May 7, 1933, in Pittsburgh, Pennsylvania. When Johnny was five, his father died, and he was raised by his mother. She instilled in him a great work ethic, which he carried with him for the rest of his life. Johnny went

to college at the University of Louisville, where he played quarterback. In 1955, he was drafted by the Pittsburgh Steelers but was released prior to the start of the season. Johnny returned home and played semi-pro football for the Bloomfield Rams before the Baltimore Colts signed him as an alternate for the 1956 season. He soon became the Colts number-one quarterback and was named the NFL's most valuable player in 1957, a distinction he would win two more times—in 1964 and 1967.

Johnny won two NFL championships with the Colts (in 1958 and 1959) and one Super Bowl (in 1971). Because of his amazing performance in the 1958 championship game (completing 26 of 40 passes for a total of 349 yards), which went into sudden-death overtime, Johnny is credited with taking American professional football from a ho-hum sport to a must-see experience. The 1958 game is often referred to as "the greatest game ever played."

Over the course of his illustrious career, Johnny threw 5,186 passes, completing 2,830, for a total of 40,239 yards and 290 touchdowns. He also set a record by throwing at least one touchdown in each of 47 consecutive games, and by the time he retired he held a total of 22 NFL passing records. Johnny was named the Greatest Quarterback of All Time in 1969, on the NFL's 50th anniversary, and in 1994 earned a place on the NFL's 75th Anniversary All-Time Team. He was elected to the Pro Football Hall of Fame in 1979, and his number, 19, has been retired by the Colts (who have since moved to Indianapolis). He died in September 2002.

SOURCES
The author referred to the following sources while researching this story.

Books

Barron, Bill, et al. *The Official NFL Encyclopedia of Pro Football.* New York: NAL Books, 1977.

Beckett, James. *Official 1992 Price Guide to Football Cards.* 11th ed. New York: House of Collectibles, 1992.

Bradshaw, Terry, with Buddy Martin. *Looking Deep.* New York: Berkley Books, 1991.

Carroll, Bob. *When The Grass Was Real: Unitas, Brown, Lombardi, Sayers, Butkus, Namath, and All the Rest; The Best Ten Years of Pro Football.* New York: Simon & Schuster, 1993.

Cohen, Richard, et al. *The Scrapbook History of Pro Football.* New York: Bobbs-Merrill, 1976.

Donovan, Arthur, Jr., and Bob Drury. *Fatso: Football When Men Were Really Men.* New York: Avon Books, 1988.

Gildea, William. *When the Colts Belonged to Baltimore: A Father and a Son, a Team and a Time.* New York: Ticknor & Fields, 1994.

Klein, Dave. *The Game of Their Lives.* New York: Random House, 1976.

Lazenby, Roland. *The Best There Ever Was: Johnny Unitas.* Chicago: Triumph Books, 2003.

Lazenby, Roland. *100 Greatest Quarterbacks.* London: Bison Books, 1988.

McDonell, Chris, ed. *The Football Game I'll Never Forget: 100 NFL Stars' Stories.* Buffalo: Firefly Books, 2004.

McDonough, Will, et al. *75 Seasons: The Complete Story of the National Football League, 1920–1995.* Atlanta: Turner, 1994.

McMahon, Jim, with Bob Verdi. *McMahon.* New York: Warner Books, 1987.

National Football League, 2005 NFL Record & Fact Book. New York: Sports Illustrated, 2005.

Sahadi, Lou. *Johnny Unitas: America's Quarterback.* Chicago: Triumph Books, 2004.

Schoor, Gene. *Bart Starr: A Biography.* Garden City, NY: Doubleday, 1977.

Sporting News. *Sporting News Selects Pro Football's Greatest Quarterbacks.* Chesterfield, MO: Sporting News, 2005.

Staubach, Roger, with Frank Luksa. *Time Enough to Win.* New York: Warner Books, 1981.

Unitas, Johnny, and Ed Fitzgerald. *The Johnny Unitas Story.* New York: Tempo Books, 1968.

Magazines

Sport, December 1958, December 1960, and August 1963.

Sports Illustrated, September 23, 2002.

DVDs

Greatest Sports Legends: Football. Eugene, OR: Marathon Music & Video, 2001.

The Complete History of the New York Giants. New York: NFL Productions and Warner Home Video, 2004.

Guides

Indianapolis Colts Football Media Guide, 1988.

New York Giants Official Information Guide, 1993.